CW00958082

IT TAKES TWO

EGMONT

We bring stories to life

First published in Great Britain 2008
by Egmont UK Limited
239 Kensington High Street, London W8 6SA

Text by Anna Bowles
Design by Claire Hammond

ISBN 978 1 4052 3810 6
1 3 5 7 9 10 8 6 4 2

Printed in Malaysia

IT TAKES TWO

EGMONT

A good friend will bring you out of your shell.

**Don't waste time
scanning the horizon
when all you need is
right under your nose.**

It's a good sign for your friendship if you can't stop rabbiting.

Show your appreciation in inventive ways.

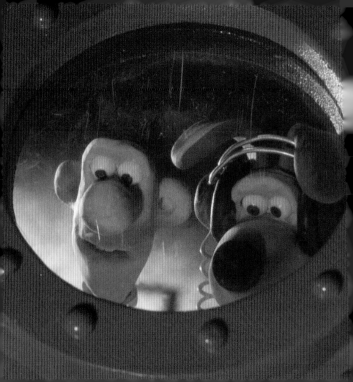

A true friend will follow you anywhere.

**Follow your dreams
or come down to Earth?
There's room for both
approaches.**

Rely on your friend,
but never assume
they've packed
the parachutes.

Counting Down in the Tottington Hall Giant Vegetable Competition - only five days of growing left. Visit our special stall on the day for great giveaways and growing tips

THE MORNING POST

THE PAPER WITH IT'S FINGER ON THE PULSES

3c

HUMANE PEST CONTROL TRIUMPHS AGAIN

RABBIT PROBLEM CONTAINED

A WEEE reign of rebel of mind not right in and get rated regain. 100's POST avenged a falling master of a local gennner getted harvest.

Marrow escape for gardener

With a screech of brakes and a damned roll, the experts from Anti-Pesto Humane Pest Control saved the day again when they heroically thwarted the dastardly rabbit raised on devouring a local master's mush breed marrow.

HEROS

REG AMENDMENT
To the Another

RABBIT

PROTECTION

Always share the glory.

It's great when
your friend is
truly your equal.

Having a friend means having a back-up plan.

Teamwork can
be glamorous
and exciting.
Also, cold and damp.

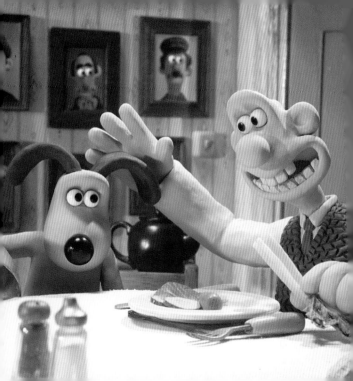

Encourage your friend to make healthy lifestyle choices.

Don't be afraid to speak out if your friend's behaviour becomes disturbing.

Friends stick together through all the ups and downs.

It's the simple things
that cement
a friendship.

**Work together,
but keep your roles
clearly defined.**

Whatever happens, you're in it together.

Someone needs to be in the driving seat of any relationship. Preferably someone who knows where they are going.

A good friend will catch
you when you fall.

Relying entirely on your own judgement is unwise.

Remember to take your friend's interests into account when selecting shared activities.

Shared interests can strengthen your relationship.

It's not disloyal
to occasionally
be embarrassed
by someone you love.

In any relationship, try to avoid asking for the moon on a stick.

There's no substitute for that one special person.

Friendship is the willingness to pull one of Wallace's homemade crackers.

**Two's company.
Three is cause
to growl.**

When fame beckons,
a true friend will
help keep your
head screwed on.

If someone comes between you, chase them out of town!

A meeting of mugs
is a meeting of minds.